Dear Parents:

Congratulations! Your child is taking the first steps on an exciting journey. The destination? Independent reading!

STEP INTO READING® will help your child get there. The program offers five steps to reading success. Each step includes fun stories and colorful art or photographs. In addition to original fiction and books with favorite characters, there are Step into Reading Non-Fiction Readers, Phonics Readers and Boxed Sets, Sticker Readers, and Comic Readers—a complete literacy program with something to interest every child.

Learning to Read, Step by Step!

Ready to Read   Preschool–Kindergarten
• big type and easy words • rhyme and rhythm • picture clues
For children who know the alphabet and are eager to begin reading.

Reading with Help   Preschool–Grade 1
• basic vocabulary • short sentences • simple stories
For children who recognize familiar words and sound out new words with help.

Reading on Your Own   Grades 1–3
• engaging characters • easy-to-follow plots • popular topics
For children who are ready to read on their own.

Reading Paragraphs   Grades 2–3
• challenging vocabulary • short paragraphs • exciting stories
For newly independent readers who read simple sentences with confidence.

Ready for Chapters   Grades 2–4
• chapters • longer paragraphs • full-color art
For children who want to take the plunge into chapter books but still like colorful pictures.

STEP INTO READING® is designed to give every child a successful reading experience. The grade levels are only guides; children will progress through the steps at their own speed, developing confidence in their reading.

Remember, a lifetime love of reading starts with a single step!

Step into Reading, Random House, and the Random House colophon are registered trademarks of Penguin Random House LLC.

Visit us on the Web!
StepIntoReading.com
rhcbooks.com

Educators and librarians, for a variety of teaching tools, visit us at RHTeachersLibrarians.com

ISBN 978-0-593-57131-6 (trade) — ISBN 978-0-593-57132-3 (lib. bdg.)
ISBN 978-0-593-57133-0 (ebook)

Printed in the United States of America
10 9 8 7 6 5 4 3 2 1

2022 Random House Children's Books Edition

©MGA

BE YOU!

by B.B. Arthur

Random House 🏠 New York

In the L.O.L. Surprise squad,
everyone is different.
They love it!

Being different
makes them who they are.

Even when friends
are as different as
Yin and Yang,
they find balance—together.

ABCD

Some friends want to wear
every bright color they can find.

Some prefer black and white.

Both Neon Q.T. and

Beatnik Babe rock their styles!

Some friends can be tough,
and some can be dainty.

Both Tough Guy
and Grand Queen
love to be themselves.

Some friends like to rock out to metal. Others love the twang of country.

Metal Babe and Twang agree
that they both love music!

Some friends have short hair,
and some have long hair.

©MGA

Crop it low,
or let it grow—
all hair is beautiful!

©MGA

Curly, wavy, and straight hair,
pulled into a puff
or woven into braids—
every style is possible.
Every style is fab, too!

17

This squad rocks
all skin tones.
They are all different,
and they all feel strong
in their skin.

18

©MGA

Friends have brown eyes,
blue eyes, green eyes—
every color!

Their eyes sparkle
like sequins when
they smile.

Some friends wear glasses.
Glasses may look fierce,
but they also help
these queens see
their fab friends.

22

23

©MGA

Friends have
different hobbies.
Grow Grrrl likes to garden outside.

Tech Girl would rather be inside
on her computer.

Both believe in chasing
their passions!

Honey Bun likes a low-key style.

26

Her Majesty loves to be extra!
These good friends stay true
to themselves even though
they are different.

©MGA

Shiny Baybay likes sunny days.

Rain Q.T. likes rainy days.

Every person is different,

just like every day.

This squad can be as different

as punk and pop,

neon and pastel,

or fire and water.

But one thing stays the same. . . .

They are friends forever!

©MGA